William Heinemann Ltd
an imprint of Reed Consumer Books Limited
Michelin House, 81 Fulham Road, London SW3 6RB
and Auckland, Melbourne, Singapore and Toronto
First published 1991
Reprinted 1992, 1993
Copyright © Allan Ahlberg and Janet Ahlberg 1991
The right of Allan Ahlberg and Janet Ahlberg to be
identified as author and illustrator of this work has
been asserted by them in accordance with the
Copyright, Designs and Patents Act 1988

Consultant Designer: Douglas Martin

0 434 92532 2
Produced by Mandarin Offset
Printed and bound in Singapore

Janet and Allan Ahlberg

The Jolly Christmas Postman

HEINEMANN · LONDON

Once upon a Christmas Eve
  Just after it had snowed,
The Jolly Postman (him again!)
  Came down the jolly road;
And in the bag upon his back
  An ... *interesting* load.

First stop: Four Bears Cottage.

A Christmas card for Baby Bear,
  A babier bear who's shy.
A mummy up a ladder;
  A postman with a pie.
A postman on his bike again:
  Ta, ta! Take care! Bye-bye!

The Jolly Postman cycles on;
  He sees three fiddlers playing;
The fast-eloping dish and spoon;
  The mighty beanstalk swaying;
The seven dwarfs upon the hill;
  The jolly snowmen sleighing.

And, by and by, second stop,
He comes to Red Riding Hood's house.

FIRST CLASS

WOBBLETON
22 XII 1988
1130 AM

POST EARLY
FOR
CHRISTMAS

19

MISS R. HOOD
THE PLAY HOUSE
GARDEN PATH
DIDDLE DUMPLING

A jolly game – a lucky girl!
 But see what's written here:
'From Mr Wolf' – he's got a nerve –
 'A Merry Christmas, dear'!
The Postman can't think what to say,
 And sips his ginger beer,

          … And eats his pie,
           And waves bye-bye.

The Postman gets back on his bike
  And rides another mile.
A crooked mile, in actual fact,
  It takes him quite a while.
He never finds the sixpence, though,
  Or, come to that, the stile.
And, besides, the crooked man has it.

Next stop: the hospital!

Humpty Dumpty smiles and blinks.
 'A jigsaw – for me? What fun!' he thinks.
'From all the King's horses
 And all the King's men – how nice.'
Then he falls out of bed
 And gets cracked again, i.e. twice.

Never mind …
In comes the doctor (Foster),
In comes the nurse,
In comes the lady with the alligator purse
… and they mend him.

The Jolly Postman waves bye-bye;
  He still has far to go.
The sun has vanished from the sky,
  The clouds are hanging low.
He feels a 'kiss' upon his cheek –
  The first fresh flakes of snow.

And comes – number four –
To a small tin door.

PAT O'CAKE
BAKERS
WE USE JOLLY MILLER FLOUR

CROOKED MILE
1.15 PM
22 DEC
1988

THE GINGERBREAD BOY
McVITIE HOUSE
LITTLE TOE LANE
TOYTOWN.

'A book in a book!' says the Gingerbread Boy.
  'What a simply *delicious* surprise.'
(But if only he knew, *he's* in one, too –
  That really would open his eyes.)
Then ...
  A bucket of tea for the Postman
And four and twenty mince pies.

Off through the snow the Postman rides
  With more than a meal in his insides.
He's all shook up and all of a-quiver,
  And it's not just the cold that makes him shiver.
There's a letter he'd rather not deliver ...

To you-know-who.
Oooooh!

DIDDLE
1988
DEC 23
AM
DUMPLING

19

MISTER WOLF

THE
DEN

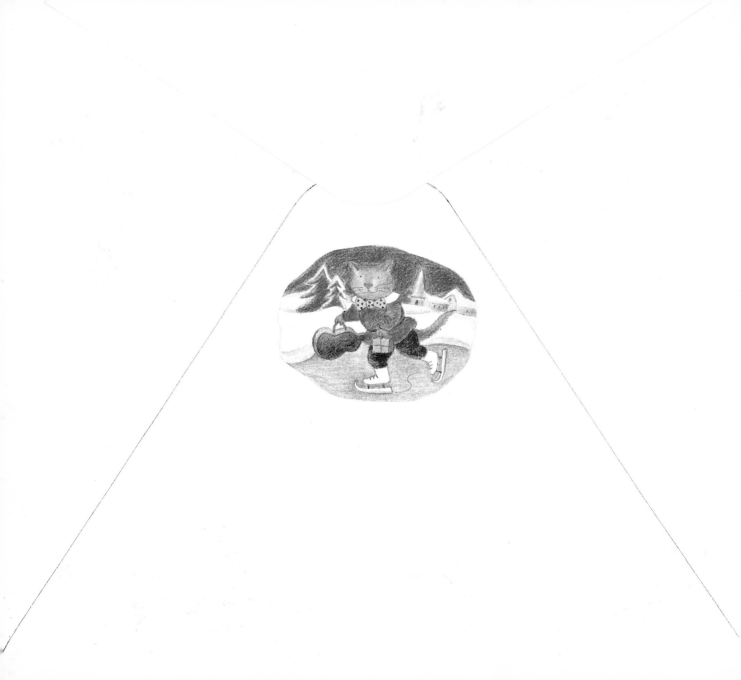

But all's well and all's merry;
  The Wolf's just wolfing pies and sherry,
And playing games in his cosy den
  ('What's the time, Mr Wolf?')
With the three little pigs
  And the little red hen.

After all, it *is* Christmas.

But now it's *really* snowing,
  And the winter wind is blowing,
And the daylight, it is going.
  So the Jolly Postman – jolly cold –
Has just no way of knowing
  Where he is …

He stops beside a wall of ice.
  He spies a crack of light.
He finds a little golden door …
  And disappears from sight,
Along a tunnel, dark and cool,
  To a *workshop*, warm and bright.

A cup of tea with Santa,
  And Mrs Santa, too.
'Got any *children's* letters?'
  The Postman smiles, 'A few!'
'Well, fancy that,' says Santa.
  'Now – we've got one for you!'

For our
good old pal
The Postman

Take a Peep!

A peep-show for a postman.
  The Postman peeps inside.
A postman's round completed:
  'It's time to take a ride!'
But how to make the journey?
  The drifts are deep and wide.

To avoid the snow
(Ho, ho, ho!)
p.t.o.

A Jolly Postman, warm and snug.
A postman's dog upon the rug.
A clock that's chiming in the hall.
A *Merry Christmas* – one and all!

The End